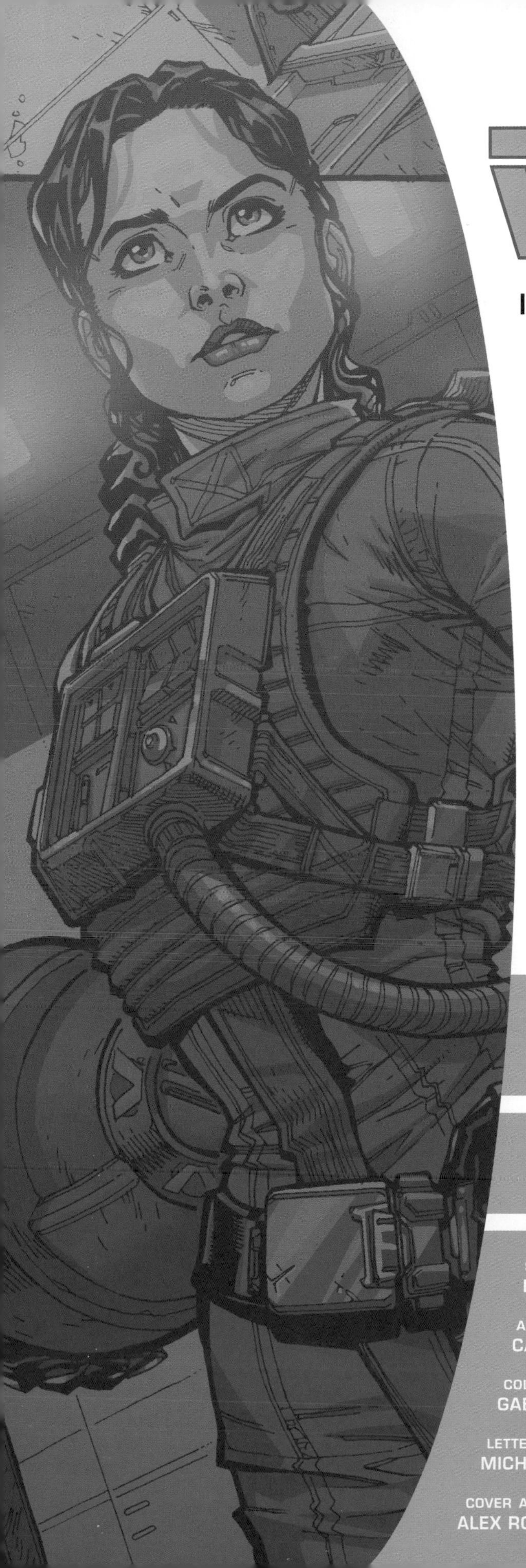

STAR WARS®

IN THE SHADOW OF YAVIN
VOLUME FOUR

As the euphoria over their destruction of the Death Star begins to wane, the realities of fighting—and surviving against—the Empire begin to take their toll on key members of the Rebel Alliance. Compounding these pressures is the suspicion of a spy in their midst.

Princess Leia risks the cohesion of her newly formed secret squadron by grounding Luke Skywalker and a female pilot, Prithi, for not taking the initial training seriously—just when the Empire is prepared to unleash Colonel Bircher and his elite squadron of TIE Interceptors.

Meanwhile, Han Solo and Chewbacca, on a supply mission for Rebel leader Mon Mothma, have run into their own Imperial troubles on Coruscant . . .

THE REBELLION
FROM THE BATTLE OF YAVIN TO FIVE YEARS AFTER

The events in this story take place shortly after the events in *Star Wars:* Episode IV—*A New Hope*.

SCRIPT
BRIAN WOOD

ART
CARLOS D'ANDA

COLORS
GABE ELTAEB

LETTERING
MICHAEL HEISLER

COVER ART
ALEX ROSS

DARK HORSE COMICS

WWW.ABDOPUBLISHING.COM

Reinforced library bound edition published in 2015 by Spotlight, a division of ABDO PO Box 398166, Minneapolis, Minnesota 55439. Spotlight produces high-quality reinforced library bound editions for schools and libraries. Published by agreement with Dark Horse Comics, Inc., and Lucasfilm Ltd.

Printed in the United States of America, North Mankato, Minnesota.
052014
072014

THIS BOOK CONTAINS
RECYCLED MATERIALS

STAR WARS: IN THE SHADOW OF YAVIN

LIBRARY OF CONGRESS CATALOGING-IN-PUBLICATION DATA

Wood, Brian, 1972-
   Star Wars : in the shadow of Yavin / writer: Brian Wood ; artist: Carlos D'Anda. -- Reinforced library bound edition.
      pages cm.
   "Dark Horse."
   "LucasFilm."
   ISBN 978-1-61479-286-4 (vol. 1) -- ISBN 978-1-61479-287-1 (vol. 2) -- ISBN 978-1-61479-288-8 (vol. 3) -- ISBN 978-1-61479-289-5 (vol. 4) -- ISBN 978-1-61479-290-1 (vol. 5) -- ISBN 978-1-61479-291-8 (vol. 6)
   1. Graphic novels. I. D'Anda, Carlos, illustrator. II. Dark Horse Comics. III. Lucasfilm, Ltd. IV. Title. V. Title: In the shadow of Yavin.
   PZ7.7.W65St 2015
   741.5'973--dc23

                              2014005383

Spotlight

A Division of ABDO
www.abdopublishing.com

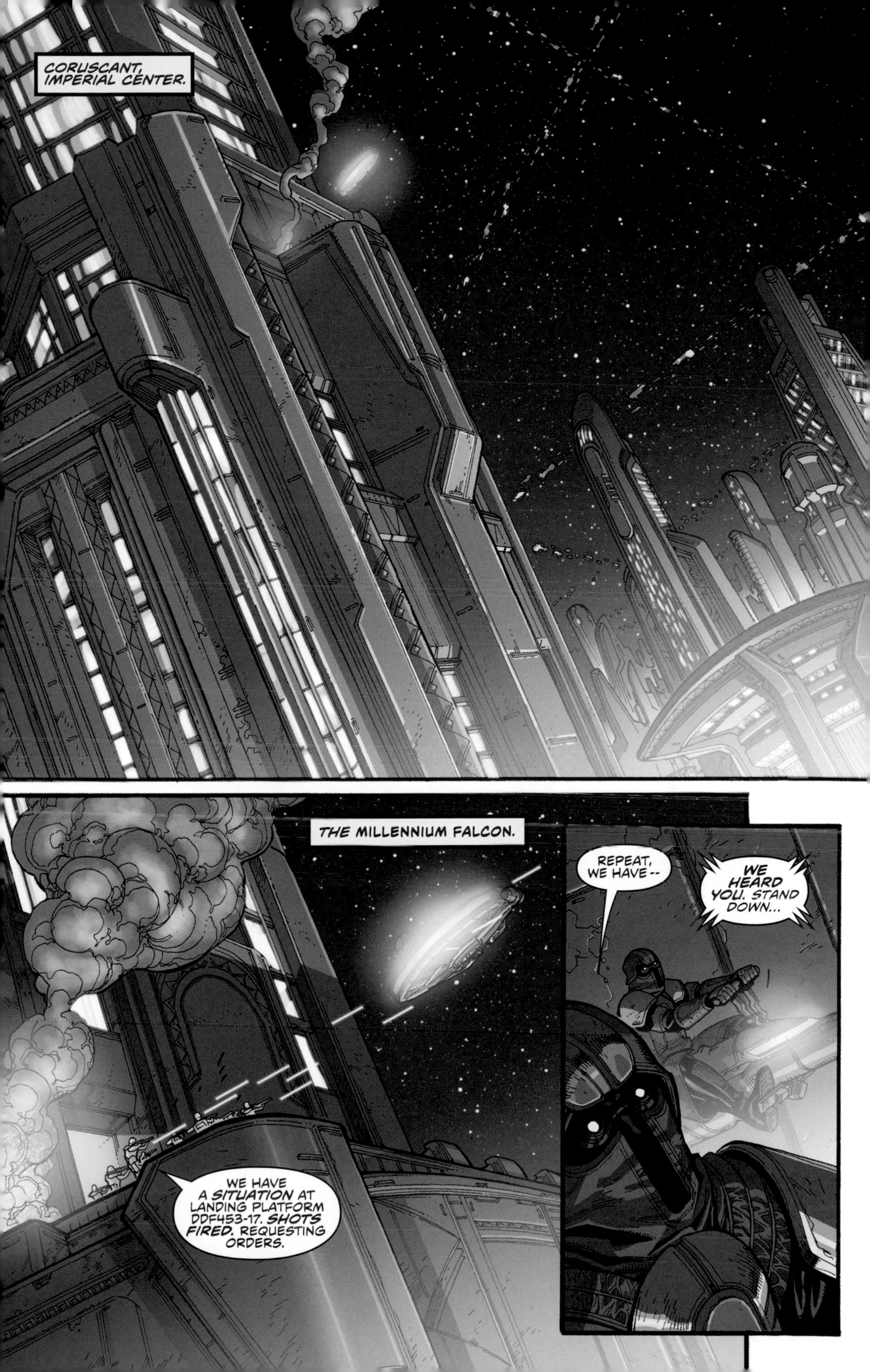
CORUSCANT, IMPERIAL CENTER.
THE MILLENNIUM FALCON.
WE HAVE A SITUATION AT LANDING PLATFORM DDF453-17. SHOTS FIRED. REQUESTING ORDERS.
REPEAT, WE HAVE --
WE HEARD YOU. STAND DOWN...

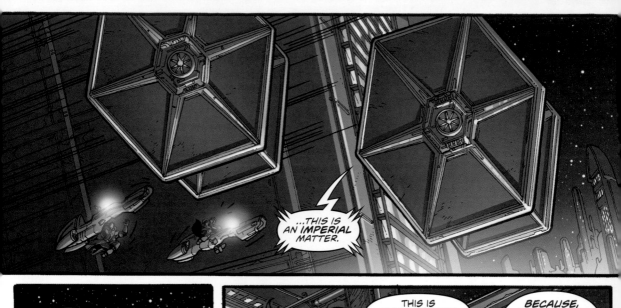

...THIS IS AN *IMPERIAL* MATTER.

WRAHH!

WHAT?

THIS IS JUST *TERRIFIC.* CHEWIE, I'M TAKING US DOWN.

WFHUA??

BECAUSE, THOSE THREE FIGHTERS BACK THERE WILL HAVE ALREADY TOLD THE *TWO DOZEN* OR SO CAPITAL SHIPS IN ORBIT THAT WE'RE HEADED THEIR WAY.

AND THAT'S *ASSUMING* WE MAKE IT PAST THE GOLAN DEFENSE NET.

I'M NO FOOL. AND BEING SNEAKY IS *WAY* UNDERRATED.

HOLD ON, CHEWIE...

...I *THINK* I REMEMBER THIS SECTOR FROM MY ACADEMY DAYS.

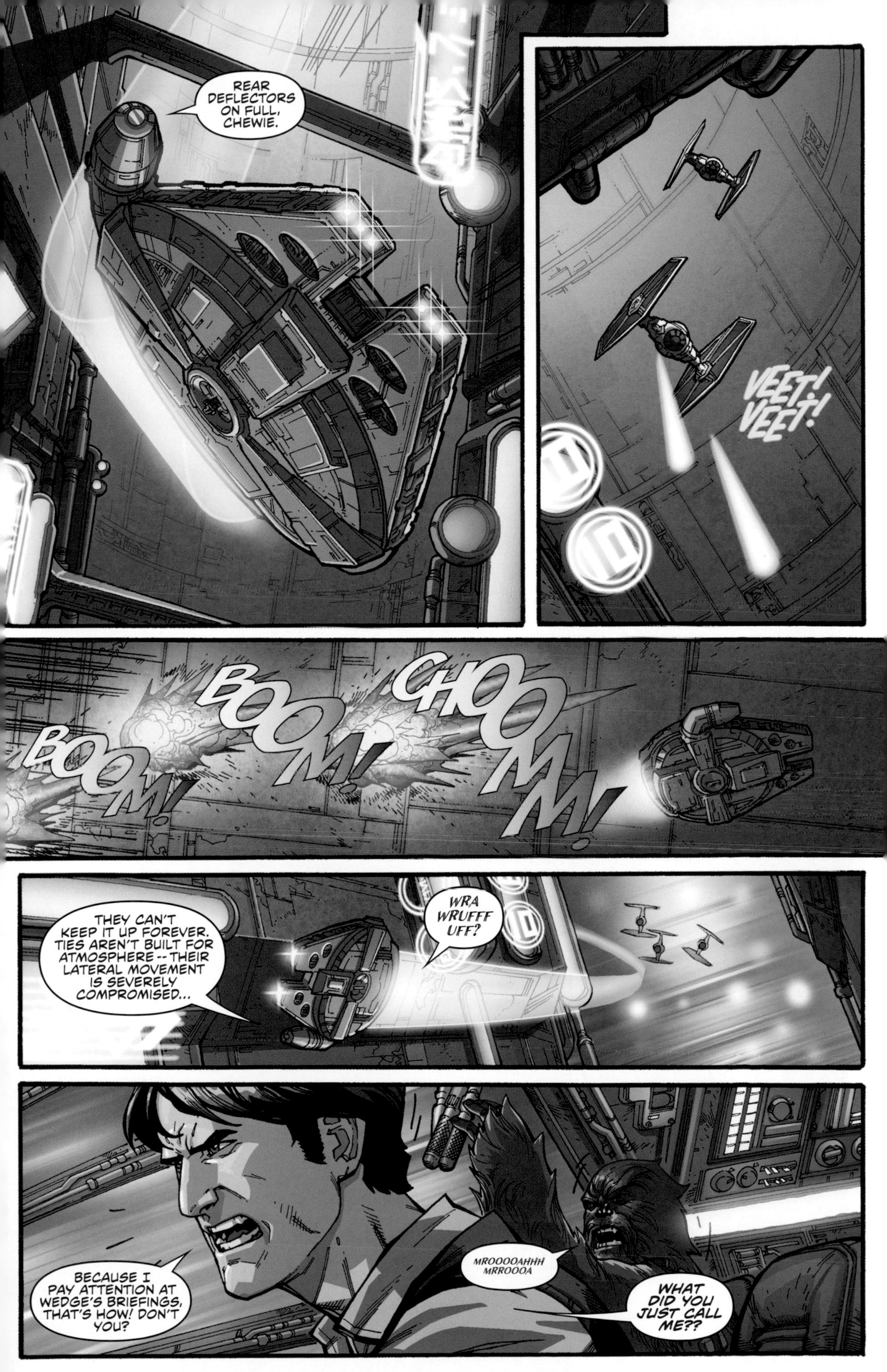
REAR DEFLECTORS ON FULL, CHEWIE.
VEET! VEET!
BOOM!
BOOM!
CHOOMM!
THEY CAN'T KEEP IT UP FOREVER. TIES AREN'T BUILT FOR ATMOSPHERE -- THEIR LATERAL MOVEMENT IS SEVERELY COMPROMISED...
WRA WRUFFF UFF?
BECAUSE I PAY ATTENTION AT WEDGE'S BRIEFINGS, THAT'S HOW! DON'T YOU?
MROOOOAHHH MRROOOA
WHAT DID YOU JUST CALL ME??

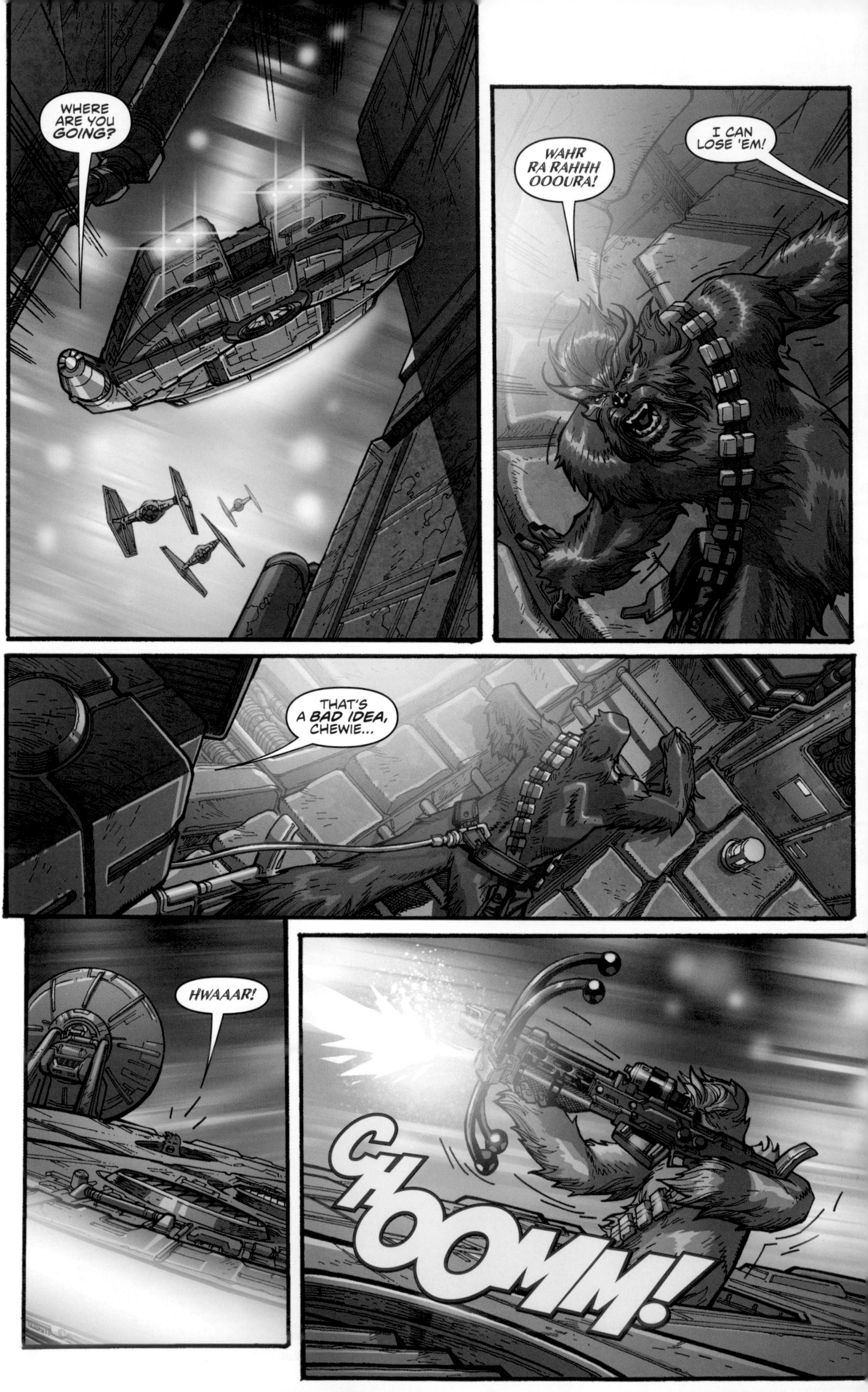

WHERE ARE YOU GOING?
WAHR RA RAHHH OOOURA!
I CAN LOSE 'EM!
THAT'S A BAD IDEA, CHEWIE...
HWAAAR!
CHOOMM!

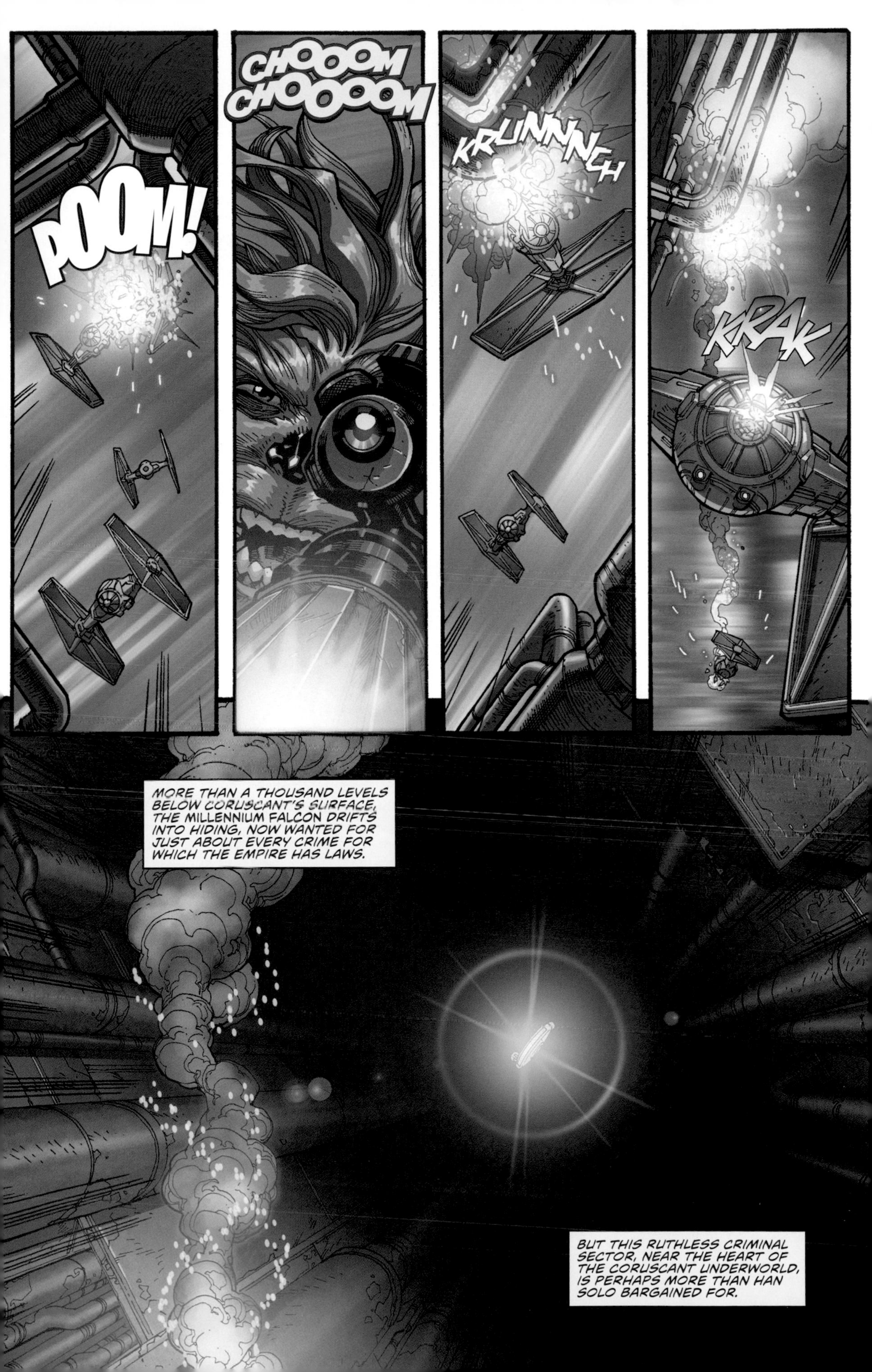
POOM!
CHOOOM CHOOOOM
KRUNNNCH
KRAK
MORE THAN A THOUSAND LEVELS BELOW CORUSCANT'S SURFACE, THE MILLENNIUM FALCON DRIFTS INTO HIDING, NOW WANTED FOR JUST ABOUT EVERY CRIME FOR WHICH THE EMPIRE HAS LAWS.
BUT THIS RUTHLESS CRIMINAL SECTOR, NEAR THE HEART OF THE CORUSCANT UNDERWORLD, IS PERHAPS MORE THAN HAN SOLO BARGAINED FOR.

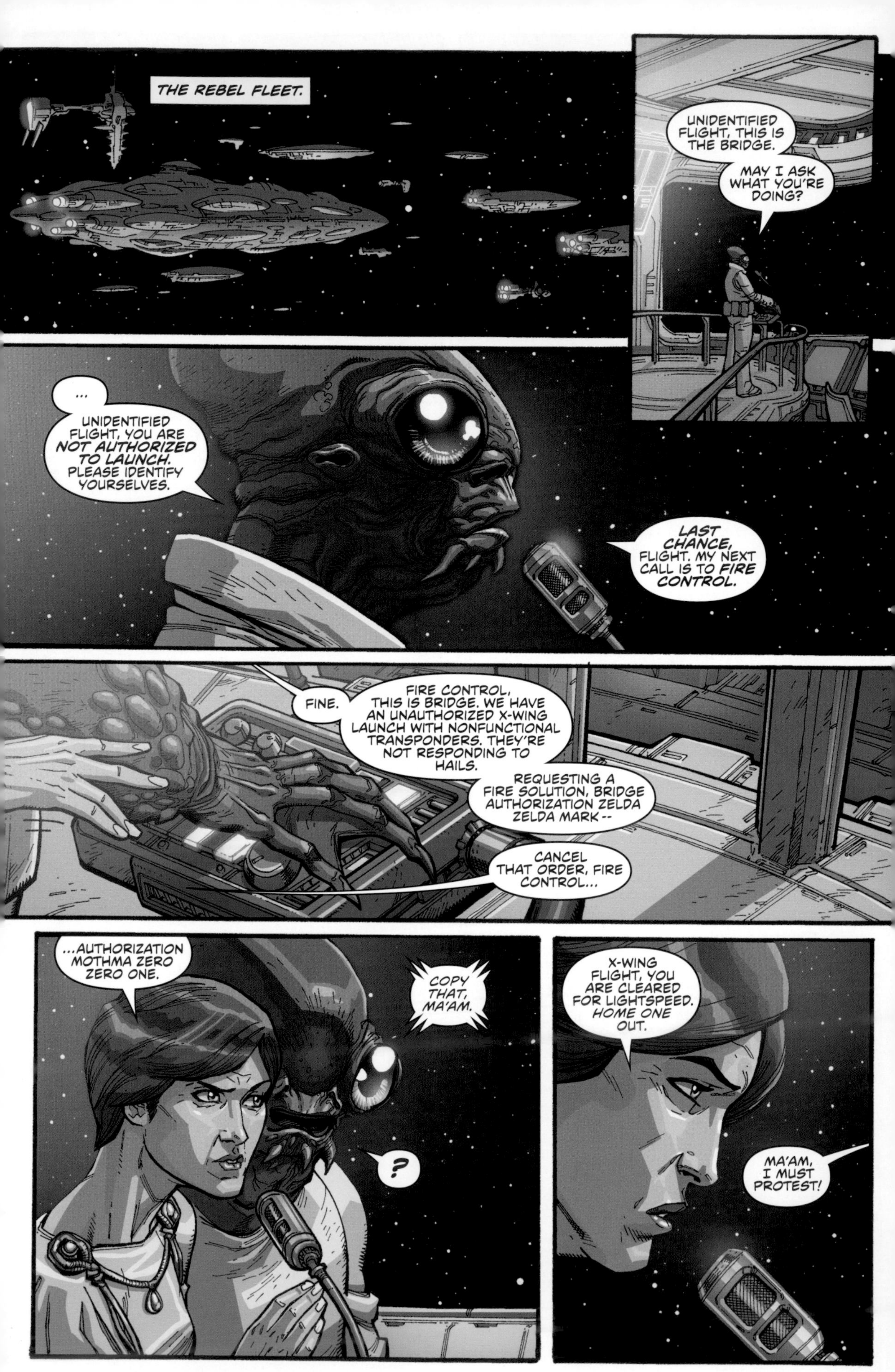
THE REBEL FLEET.
UNIDENTIFIED FLIGHT, THIS IS THE BRIDGE.
MAY I ASK WHAT YOU'RE DOING?
...
UNIDENTIFIED FLIGHT, YOU ARE NOT AUTHORIZED TO LAUNCH. PLEASE IDENTIFY YOURSELVES.
LAST CHANCE, FLIGHT. MY NEXT CALL IS TO FIRE CONTROL.
FINE.
FIRE CONTROL, THIS IS BRIDGE. WE HAVE AN UNAUTHORIZED X-WING LAUNCH WITH NONFUNCTIONAL TRANSPONDERS. THEY'RE NOT RESPONDING TO HAILS.
REQUESTING A FIRE SOLUTION, BRIDGE AUTHORIZATION ZELDA ZELDA MARK --
CANCEL THAT ORDER, FIRE CONTROL...
...AUTHORIZATION MOTHMA ZERO ZERO ONE.
COPY THAT, MA'AM.
?
X-WING FLIGHT, YOU ARE CLEARED FOR LIGHTSPEED. HOME ONE OUT.
MA'AM, I MUST PROTEST!

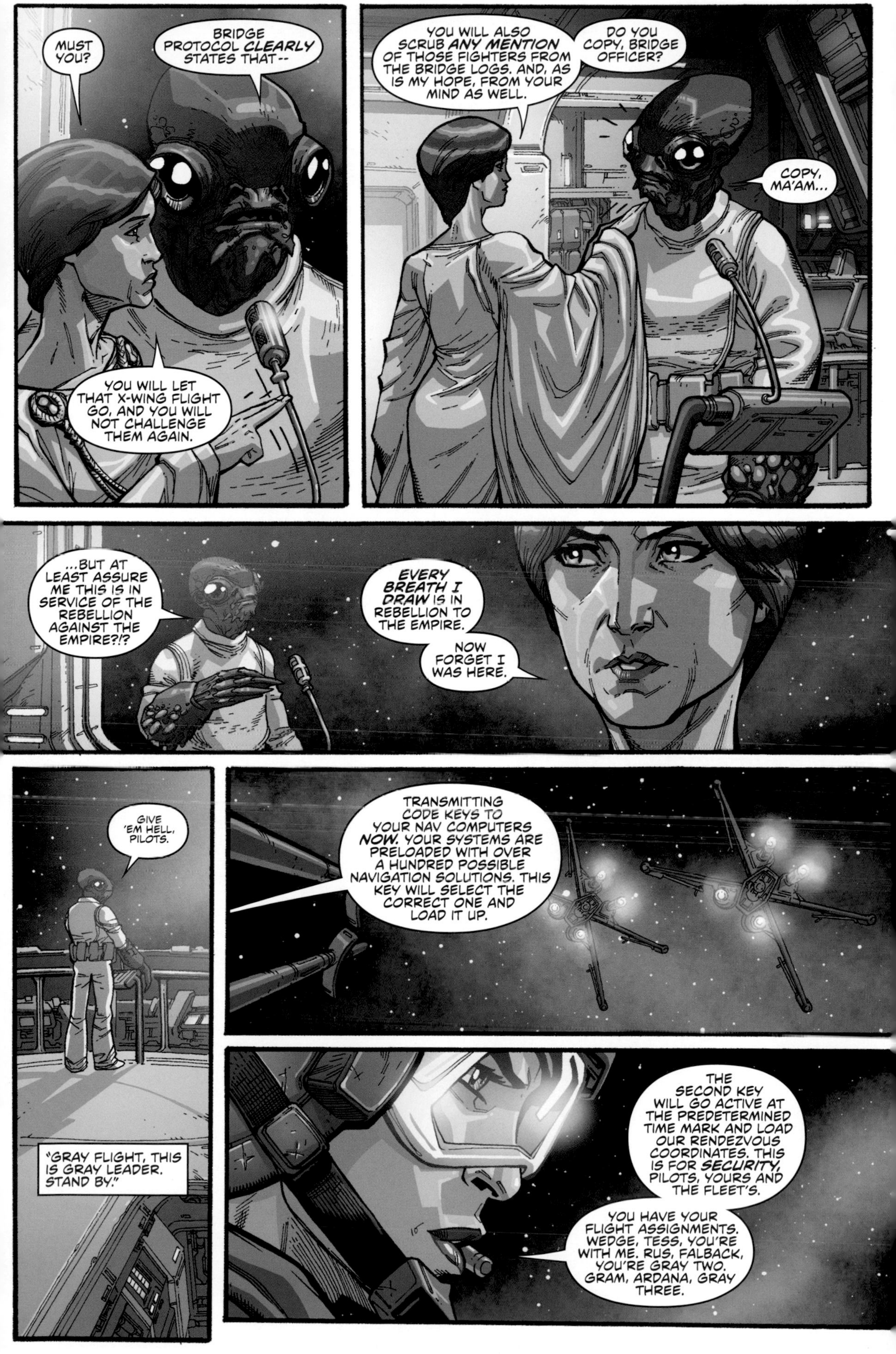
MUST YOU?
BRIDGE PROTOCOL CLEARLY STATES THAT--
YOU WILL LET THAT X-WING FLIGHT GO, AND YOU WILL NOT CHALLENGE THEM AGAIN.
YOU WILL ALSO SCRUB ANY MENTION OF THOSE FIGHTERS FROM THE BRIDGE LOGS. AND, AS IS MY HOPE, FROM YOUR MIND AS WELL.
DO YOU COPY, BRIDGE OFFICER?
COPY, MA'AM...
...BUT AT LEAST ASSURE ME THIS IS IN SERVICE OF THE REBELLION AGAINST THE EMPIRE?!?
EVERY BREATH I DRAW IS IN REBELLION TO THE EMPIRE.
NOW FORGET I WAS HERE.
GIVE 'EM HELL, PILOTS.
"GRAY FLIGHT, THIS IS GRAY LEADER. STAND BY."
TRANSMITTING CODE KEYS TO YOUR NAV COMPUTERS NOW. YOUR SYSTEMS ARE PRELOADED WITH OVER A HUNDRED POSSIBLE NAVIGATION SOLUTIONS. THIS KEY WILL SELECT THE CORRECT ONE AND LOAD IT UP.
THE SECOND KEY WILL GO ACTIVE AT THE PREDETERMINED TIME MARK AND LOAD OUR RENDEZVOUS COORDINATES. THIS IS FOR SECURITY, PILOTS, YOURS AND THE FLEET'S.
YOU HAVE YOUR FLIGHT ASSIGNMENTS. WEDGE, TESS, YOU'RE WITH ME. RUS, FALBACK, YOU'RE GRAY TWO. GRAM, ARDANA, GRAY THREE.

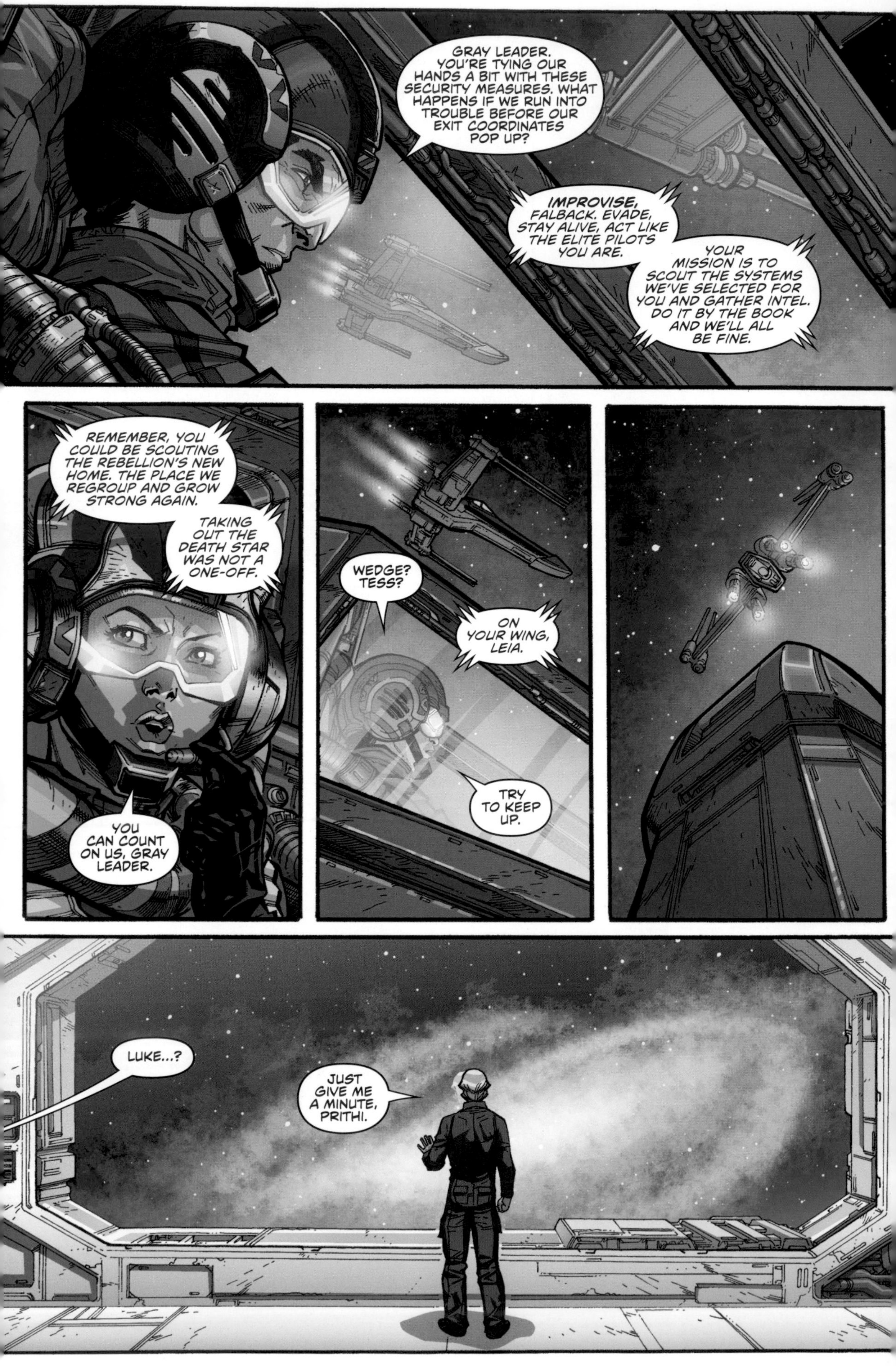
GRAY LEADER. YOU'RE TYING OUR HANDS A BIT WITH THESE SECURITY MEASURES. WHAT HAPPENS IF WE RUN INTO TROUBLE BEFORE OUR EXIT COORDINATES POP UP?
IMPROVISE, FALBACK. EVADE, STAY ALIVE, ACT LIKE THE ELITE PILOTS YOU ARE.
YOUR MISSION IS TO SCOUT THE SYSTEMS WE'VE SELECTED FOR YOU AND GATHER INTEL. DO IT BY THE BOOK AND WE'LL ALL BE FINE.
REMEMBER, YOU COULD BE SCOUTING THE REBELLION'S NEW HOME. THE PLACE WE REGROUP AND GROW STRONG AGAIN.
TAKING OUT THE DEATH STAR WAS NOT A ONE-OFF.
YOU CAN COUNT ON US, GRAY LEADER.
WEDGE? TESS?
ON YOUR WING, LEIA.
TRY TO KEEP UP.
LUKE...?
JUST GIVE ME A MINUTE, PRITHI.

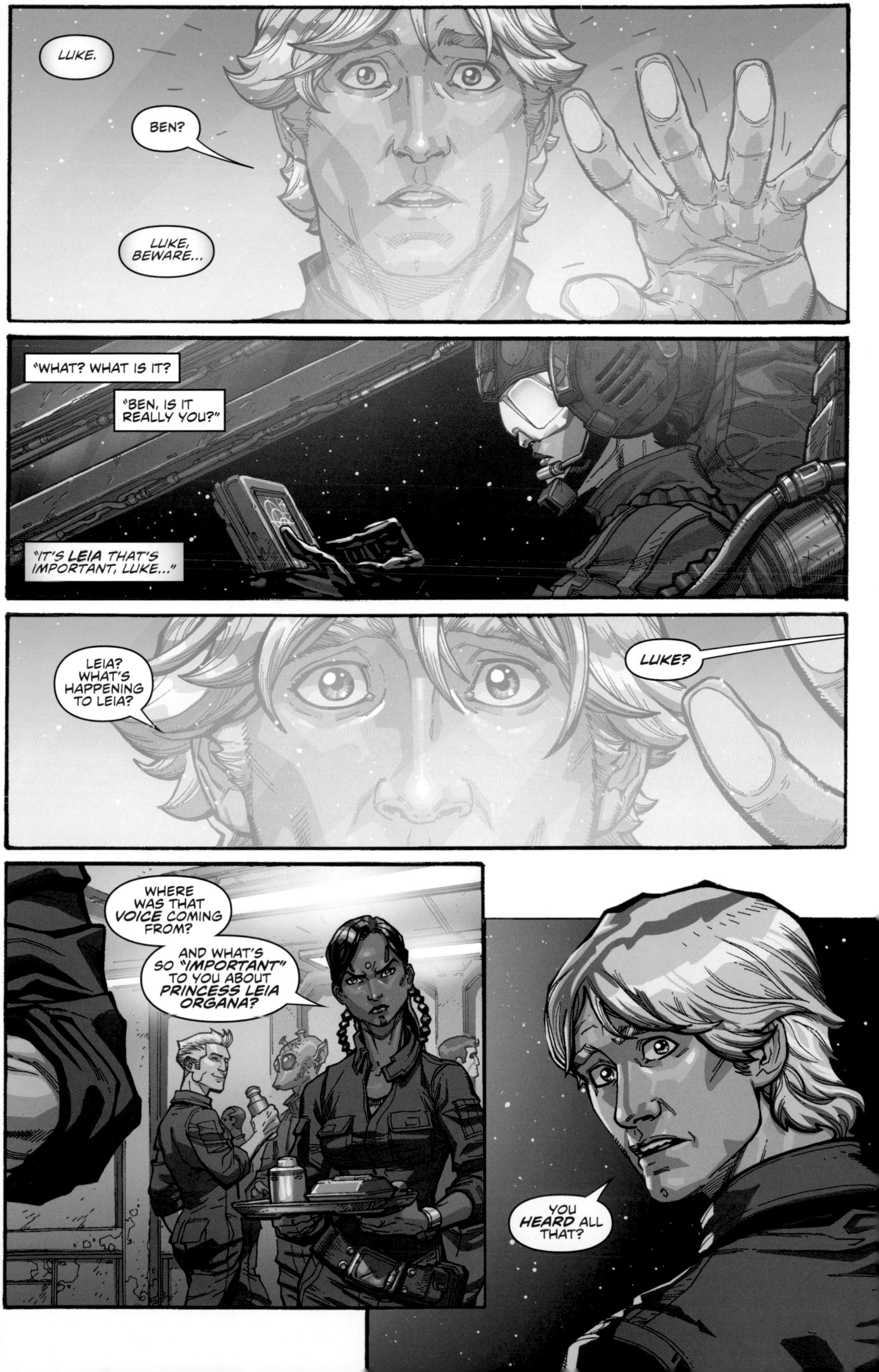
LUKE.
BEN?
LUKE, BEWARE...
"WHAT? WHAT IS IT?
"BEN, IS IT REALLY YOU?"
"IT'S LEIA THAT'S IMPORTANT, LUKE..."
LEIA? WHAT'S HAPPENING TO LEIA?
LUKE?
WHERE WAS THAT VOICE COMING FROM?
AND WHAT'S SO "IMPORTANT" TO YOU ABOUT PRINCESS LEIA ORGANA?
YOU HEARD ALL THAT?

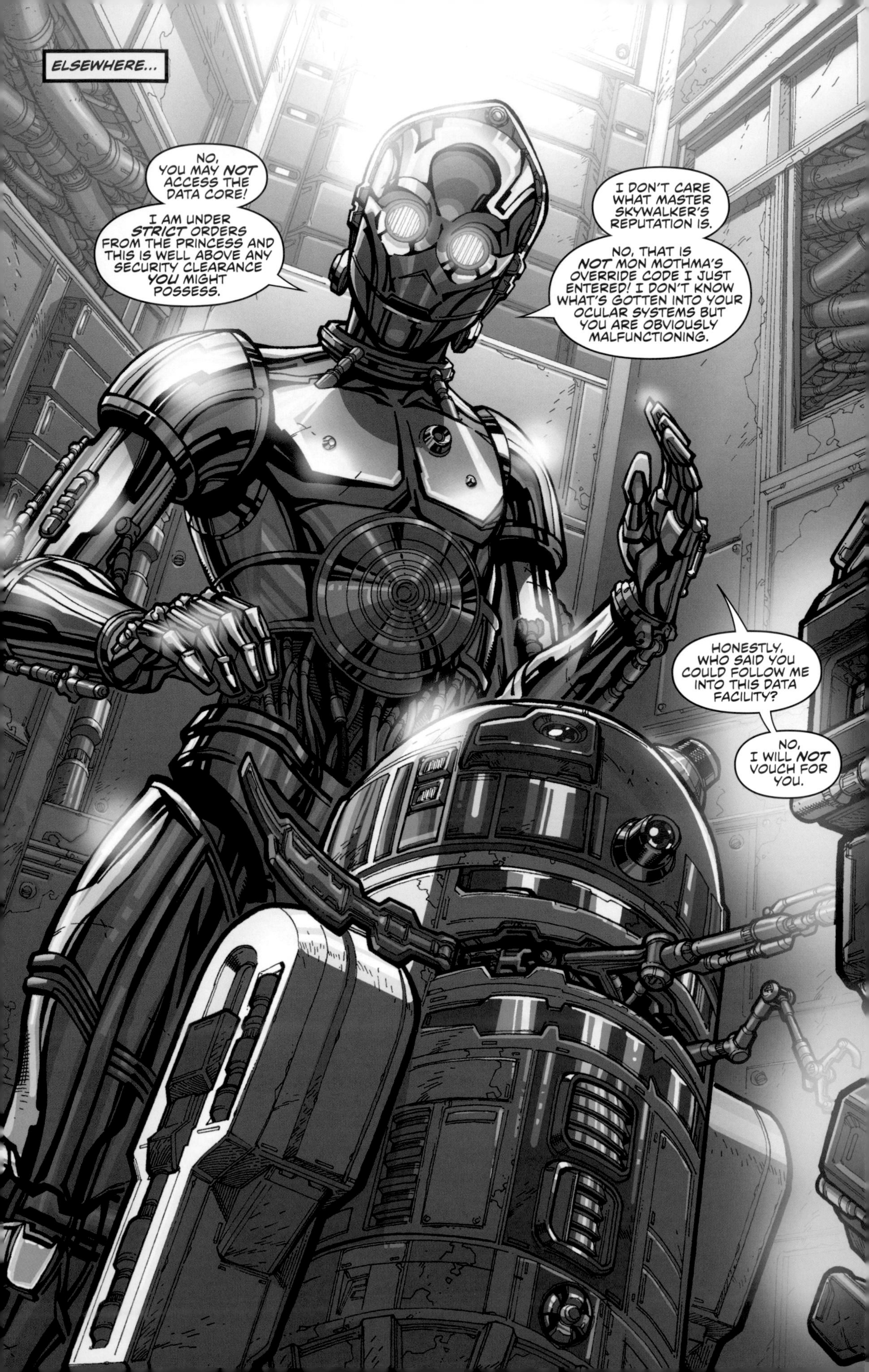
ELSEWHERE...
NO, YOU MAY NOT ACCESS THE DATA CORE!
I AM UNDER STRICT ORDERS FROM THE PRINCESS AND THIS IS WELL ABOVE ANY SECURITY CLEARANCE YOU MIGHT POSSESS.
I DON'T CARE WHAT MASTER SKYWALKER'S REPUTATION IS.
NO, THAT IS NOT MON MOTHMA'S OVERRIDE CODE I JUST ENTERED! I DON'T KNOW WHAT'S GOTTEN INTO YOUR OCULAR SYSTEMS BUT YOU ARE OBVIOUSLY MALFUNCTIONING.
HONESTLY, WHO SAID YOU COULD FOLLOW ME INTO THIS DATA FACILITY?
NO, I WILL NOT VOUCH FOR YOU.

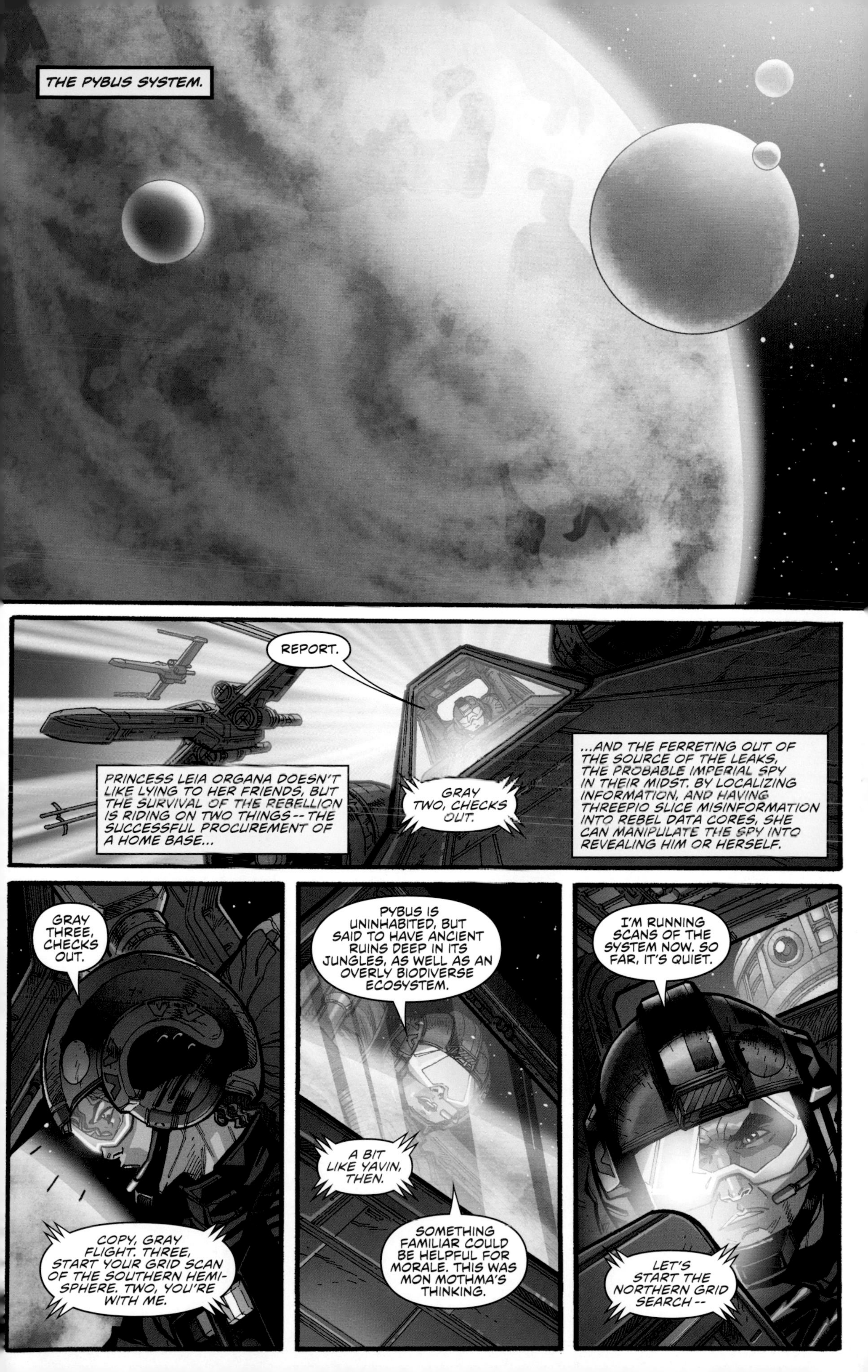
THE PYBUS SYSTEM.
REPORT.
PRINCESS LEIA ORGANA DOESN'T LIKE LYING TO HER FRIENDS, BUT THE SURVIVAL OF THE REBELLION IS RIDING ON TWO THINGS -- THE SUCCESSFUL PROCUREMENT OF A HOME BASE...
GRAY TWO, CHECKS OUT.
...AND THE FERRETING OUT OF THE SOURCE OF THE LEAKS, THE PROBABLE IMPERIAL SPY IN THEIR MIDST. BY LOCALIZING INFORMATION, AND HAVING THREEPIO SLICE MISINFORMATION INTO REBEL DATA CORES, SHE CAN MANIPULATE THE SPY INTO REVEALING HIM OR HERSELF.
GRAY THREE, CHECKS OUT.
COPY, GRAY FLIGHT. THREE, START YOUR GRID SCAN OF THE SOUTHERN HEMI-SPHERE. TWO, YOU'RE WITH ME.
PYBUS IS UNINHABITED, BUT SAID TO HAVE ANCIENT RUINS DEEP IN ITS JUNGLES, AS WELL AS AN OVERLY BIODIVERSE ECOSYSTEM.
A BIT LIKE YAVIN, THEN.
SOMETHING FAMILIAR COULD BE HELPFUL FOR MORALE. THIS WAS MON MOTHMA'S THINKING.
I'M RUNNING SCANS OF THE SYSTEM NOW. SO FAR, IT'S QUIET.
LET'S START THE NORTHERN GRID SEARCH --

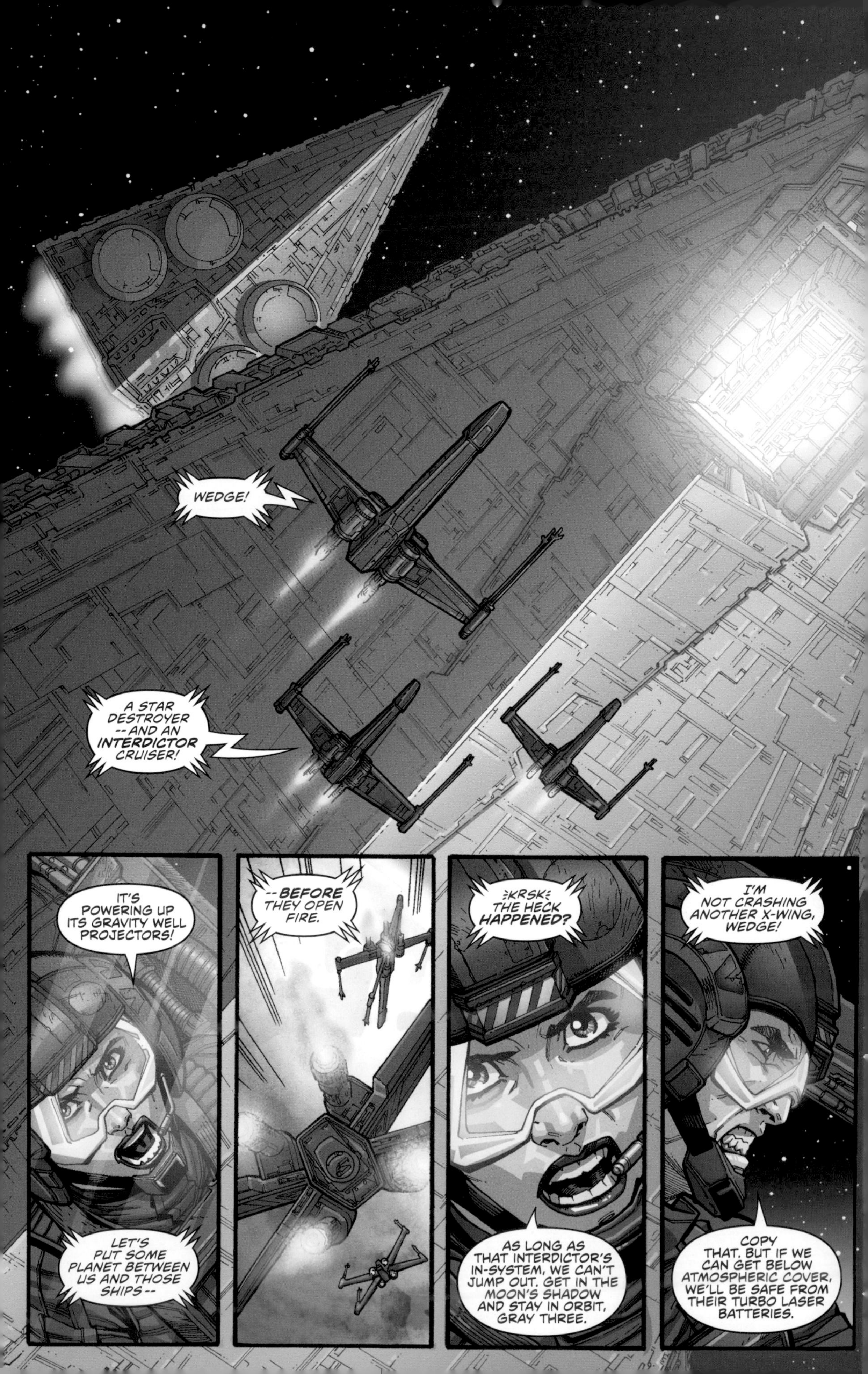
WEDGE!
A STAR DESTROYER --AND AN INTERDICTOR CRUISER!
IT'S POWERING UP ITS GRAVITY WELL PROJECTORS!
LET'S PUT SOME PLANET BETWEEN US AND THOSE SHIPS --
--BEFORE THEY OPEN FIRE.
KRSK THE HECK HAPPENED?
AS LONG AS THAT INTERDICTOR'S IN-SYSTEM, WE CAN'T JUMP OUT. GET IN THE MOON'S SHADOW AND STAY IN ORBIT, GRAY THREE.
I'M NOT CRASHING ANOTHER X-WING, WEDGE!
COPY THAT. BUT IF WE CAN GET BELOW ATMOSPHERIC COVER, WE'LL BE SAFE FROM THEIR TURBO LASER BATTERIES.

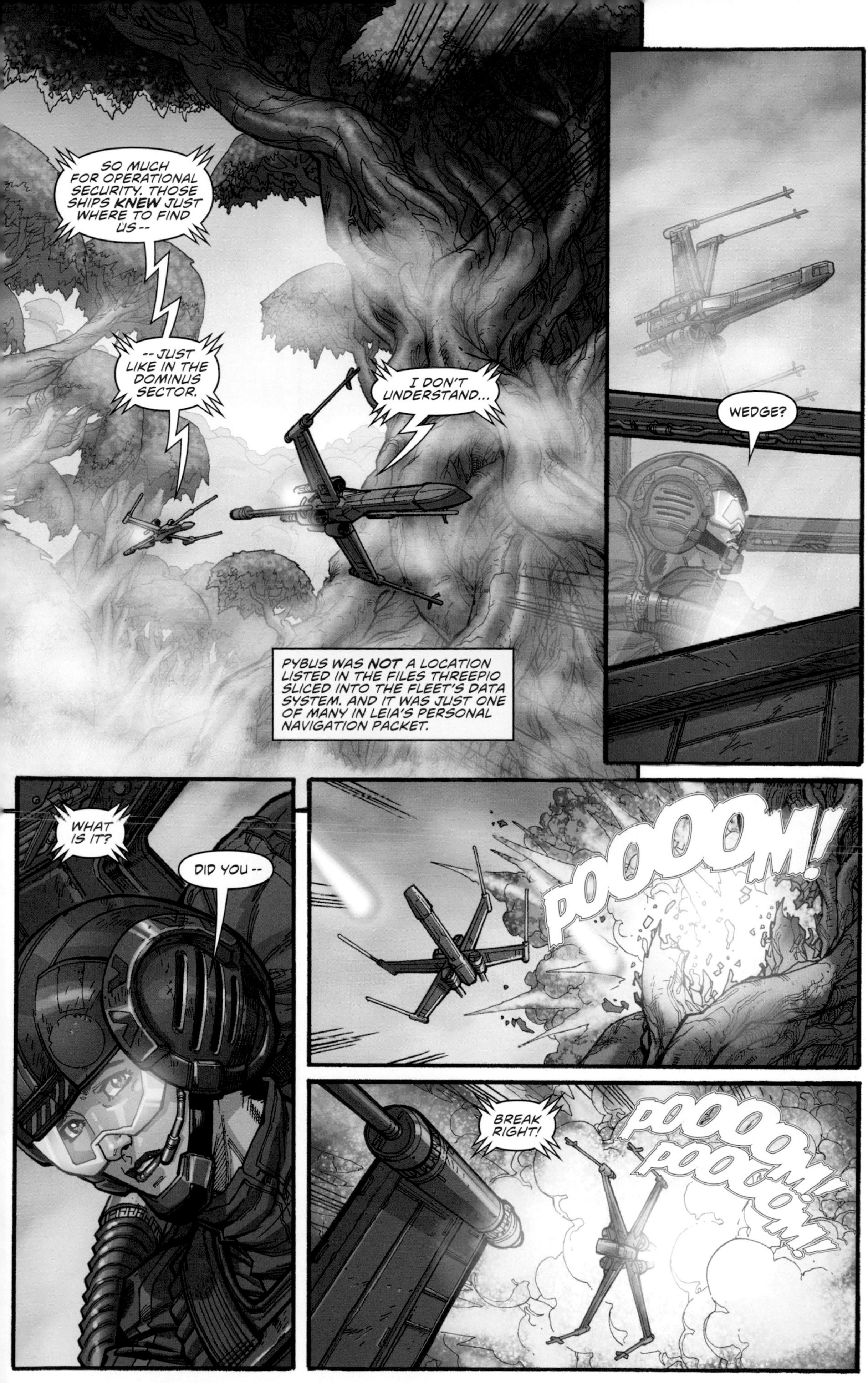
SO MUCH FOR OPERATIONAL SECURITY. THOSE SHIPS KNEW JUST WHERE TO FIND US --
-- JUST LIKE IN THE DOMINUS SECTOR.
I DON'T UNDERSTAND...
PYBUS WAS NOT A LOCATION LISTED IN THE FILES THREEPIO SLICED INTO THE FLEET'S DATA SYSTEM. AND IT WAS JUST ONE OF MANY IN LEIA'S PERSONAL NAVIGATION PACKET.
WEDGE?
WHAT IS IT?
DID YOU --
POOOOOM!
BREAK RIGHT!
POOOOM!
POOOOM!

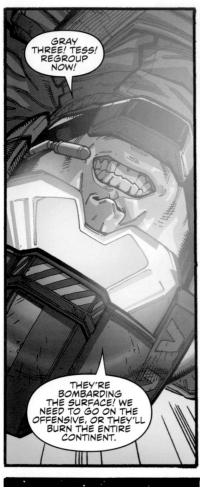

GRAY THREE! TESS! REGROUP NOW!

THEY'RE BOMBARDING THE SURFACE! WE NEED TO GO ON THE OFFENSIVE, OR THEY'LL BURN THE ENTIRE CONTINENT.

AGAINST TWO CAPITAL SHIPS?

WE KILLED A *DEATH STAR*, LEIA. GET IN UNDER THEIR SHIELDS AND INSIDE THE RANGE OF THEIR BIG GUNS. IT'S OUR ONLY SHOT.

SHIELDS FRONT FULL. GRAVITY DAMPENERS ON MAX.

THE DEATH STAR SENT DOZENS OF TIE FIGHTERS AFTER YOU, WEDGE ...DON'T FORGET ABOUT THAT.

I'LL NEVER FORGET.

INCOMING! *TWO* SQUADRONS!

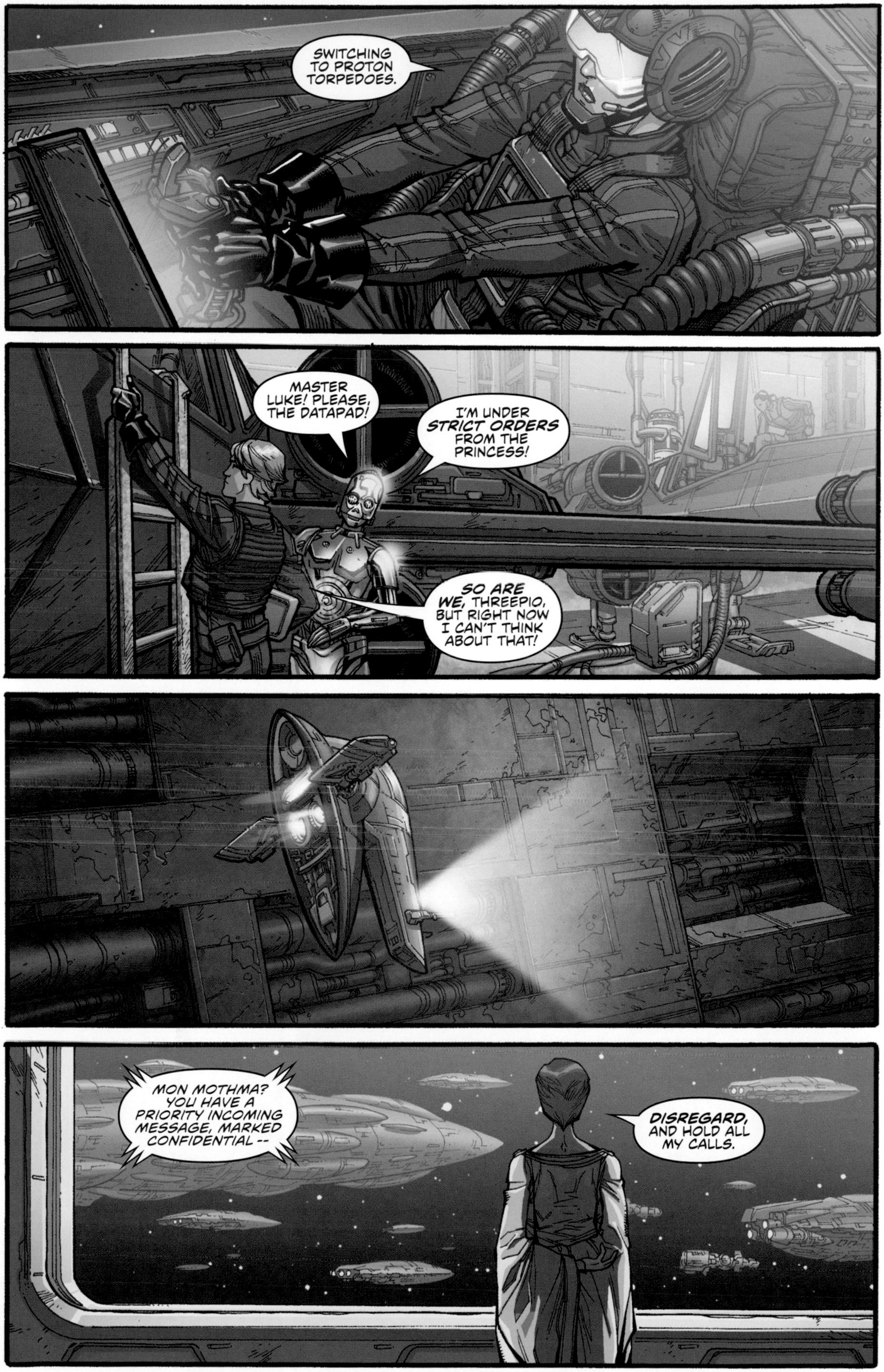
SWITCHING TO PROTON TORPEDOES.
MASTER LUKE! PLEASE, THE DATAPAD!
I'M UNDER STRICT ORDERS FROM THE PRINCESS!
SO ARE WE, THREEPIO, BUT RIGHT NOW I CAN'T THINK ABOUT THAT!
MON MOTHMA? YOU HAVE A PRIORITY INCOMING MESSAGE, MARKED CONFIDENTIAL --
DISREGARD, AND HOLD ALL MY CALLS.

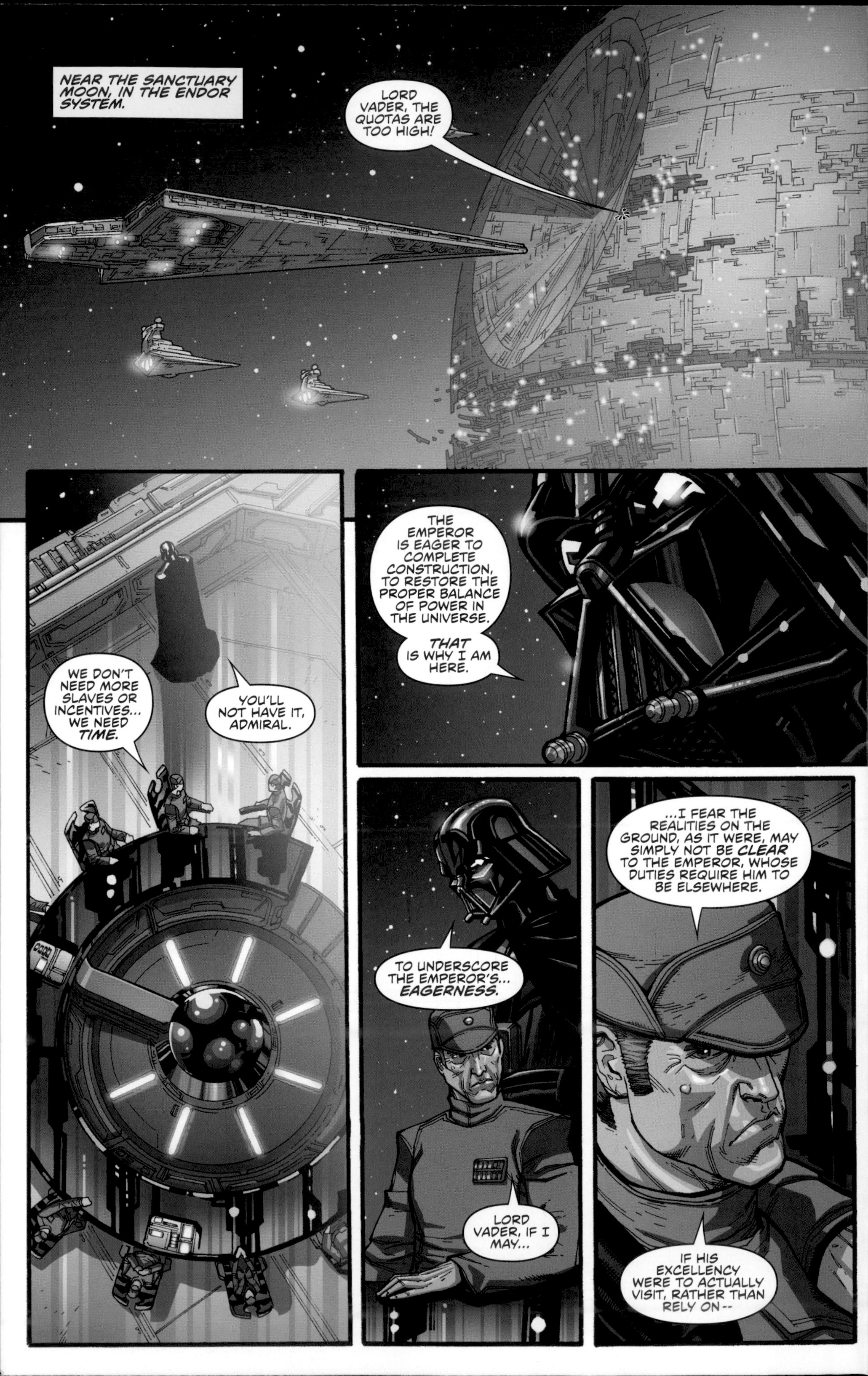
NEAR THE SANCTUARY MOON, IN THE ENDOR SYSTEM.
LORD VADER, THE QUOTAS ARE TOO HIGH!
WE DON'T NEED MORE SLAVES OR INCENTIVES... WE NEED TIME.
YOU'LL NOT HAVE IT, ADMIRAL.
THE EMPEROR IS EAGER TO COMPLETE CONSTRUCTION, TO RESTORE THE PROPER BALANCE OF POWER IN THE UNIVERSE.
THAT IS WHY I AM HERE.
TO UNDERSCORE THE EMPEROR'S... EAGERNESS.
LORD VADER, IF I MAY...
...I FEAR THE REALITIES ON THE GROUND, AS IT WERE, MAY SIMPLY NOT BE CLEAR TO THE EMPEROR, WHOSE DUTIES REQUIRE HIM TO BE ELSEWHERE.
IF HIS EXCELLENCY WERE TO ACTUALLY VISIT, RATHER THAN RELY ON--

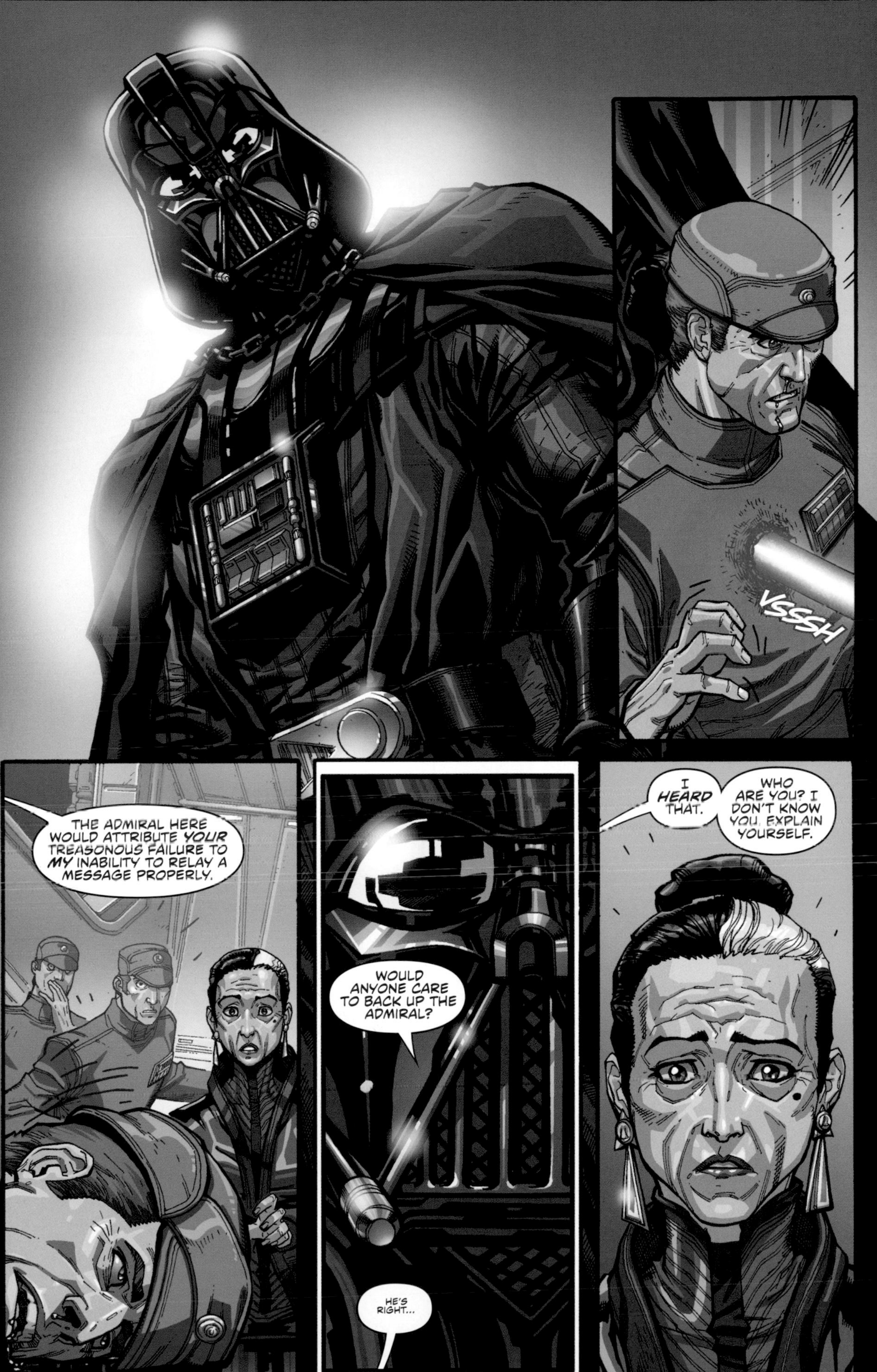
VSSSH
THE ADMIRAL HERE WOULD ATTRIBUTE YOUR TREASONOUS FAILURE TO MY INABILITY TO RELAY A MESSAGE PROPERLY.
WOULD ANYONE CARE TO BACK UP THE ADMIRAL?
HE'S RIGHT...
I HEARD THAT.
WHO ARE YOU? I DON'T KNOW YOU. EXPLAIN YOURSELF.

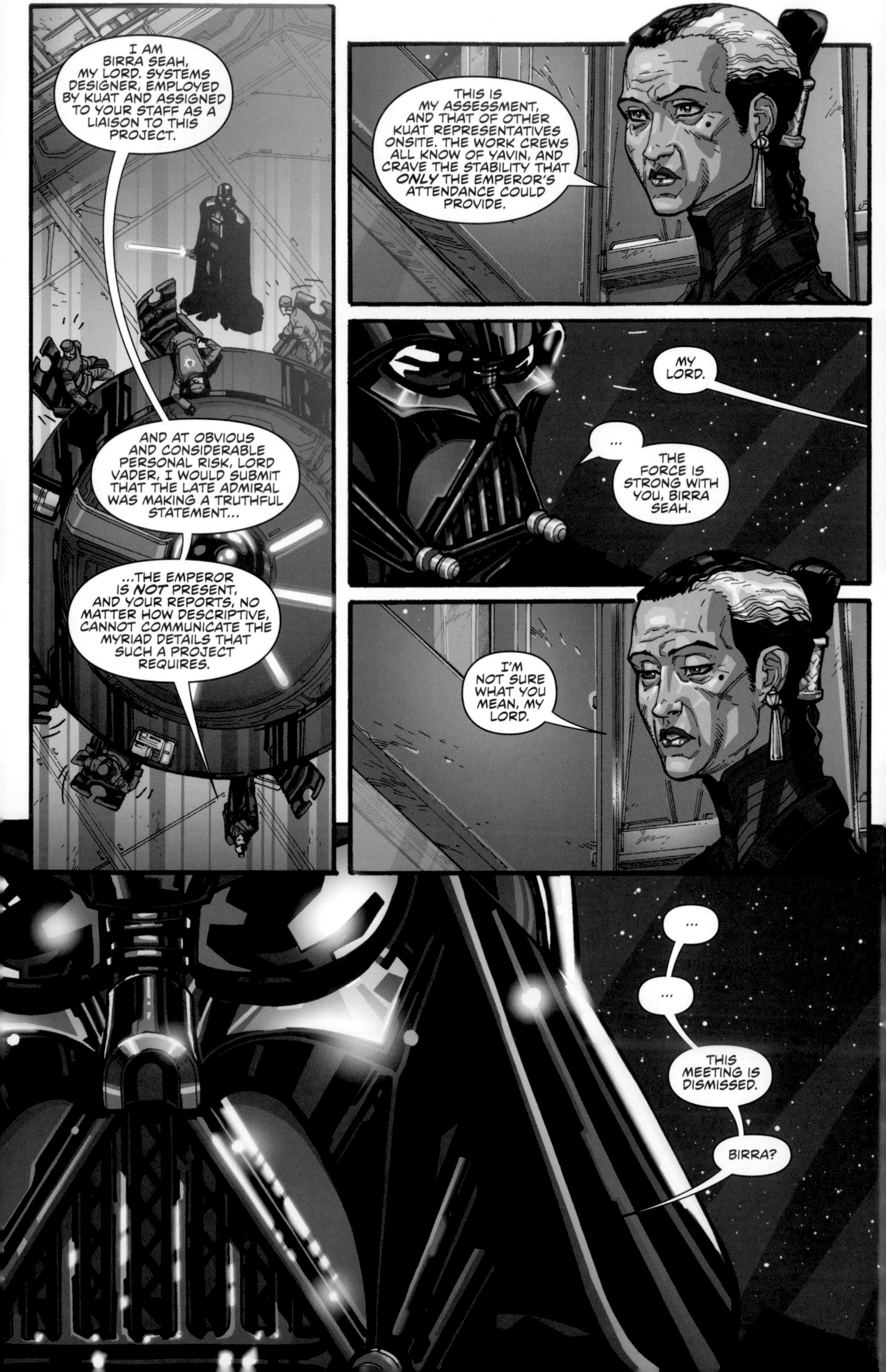
I AM BIRRA SEAH, MY LORD. SYSTEMS DESIGNER, EMPLOYED BY KUAT AND ASSIGNED TO YOUR STAFF AS A LIAISON TO THIS PROJECT.
AND AT OBVIOUS AND CONSIDERABLE PERSONAL RISK, LORD VADER, I WOULD SUBMIT THAT THE LATE ADMIRAL WAS MAKING A TRUTHFUL STATEMENT...
...THE EMPEROR IS NOT PRESENT, AND YOUR REPORTS, NO MATTER HOW DESCRIPTIVE, CANNOT COMMUNICATE THE MYRIAD DETAILS THAT SUCH A PROJECT REQUIRES.
THIS IS MY ASSESSMENT, AND THAT OF OTHER KUAT REPRESENTATIVES ONSITE. THE WORK CREWS ALL KNOW OF YAVIN, AND CRAVE THE STABILITY THAT ONLY THE EMPEROR'S ATTENDANCE COULD PROVIDE.
MY LORD.
...
THE FORCE IS STRONG WITH YOU, BIRRA SEAH.
I'M NOT SURE WHAT YOU MEAN, MY LORD.
...
...
THIS MEETING IS DISMISSED.
BIRRA?

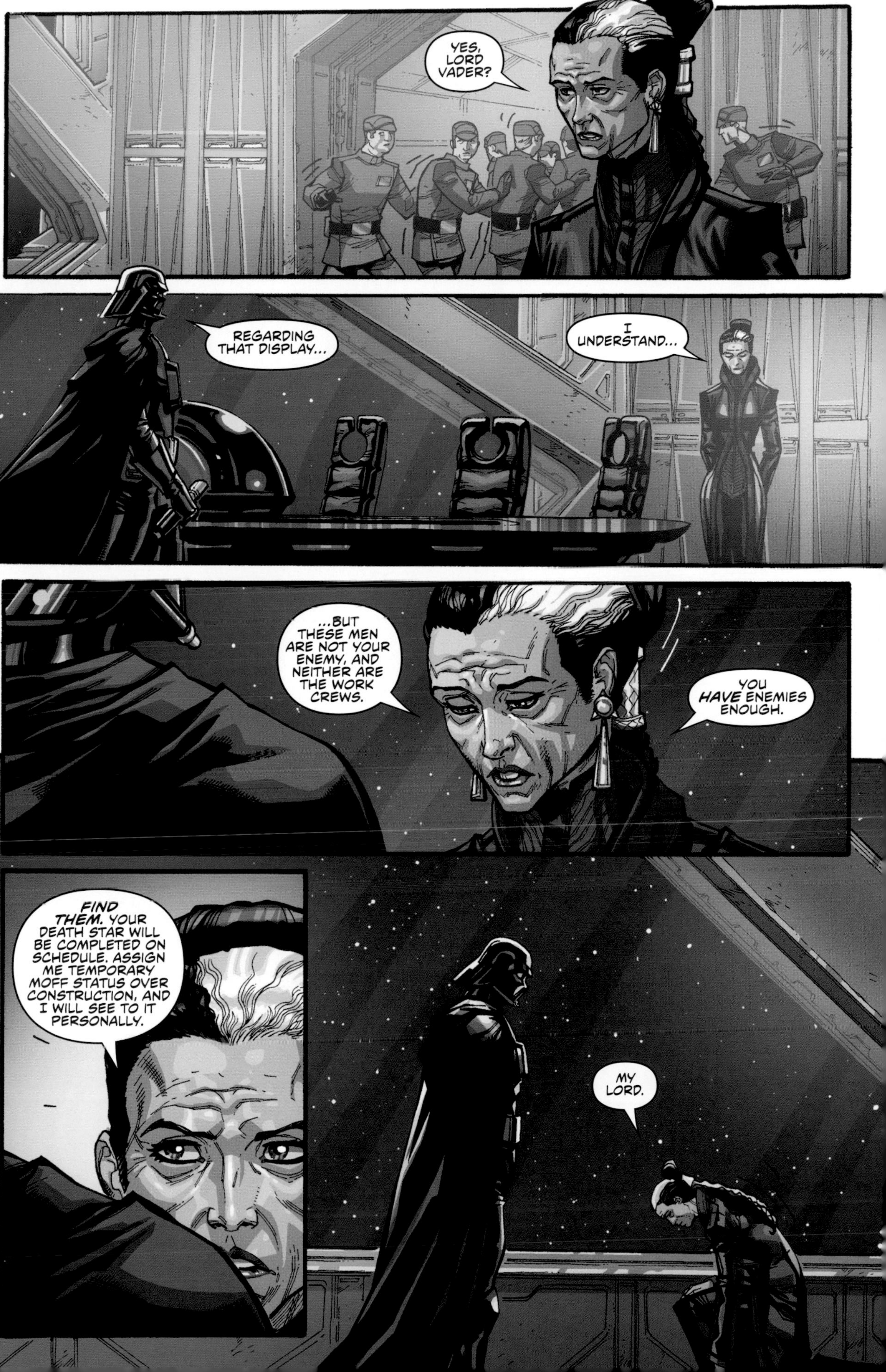
YES, LORD VADER?
REGARDING THAT DISPLAY...
I UNDERSTAND...
...BUT THESE MEN ARE NOT YOUR ENEMY, AND NEITHER ARE THE WORK CREWS.
YOU *HAVE* ENEMIES ENOUGH.
FIND THEM. YOUR DEATH STAR WILL BE COMPLETED ON SCHEDULE. ASSIGN ME TEMPORARY MOFF STATUS OVER CONSTRUCTION, AND I WILL SEE TO IT PERSONALLY.
MY LORD.

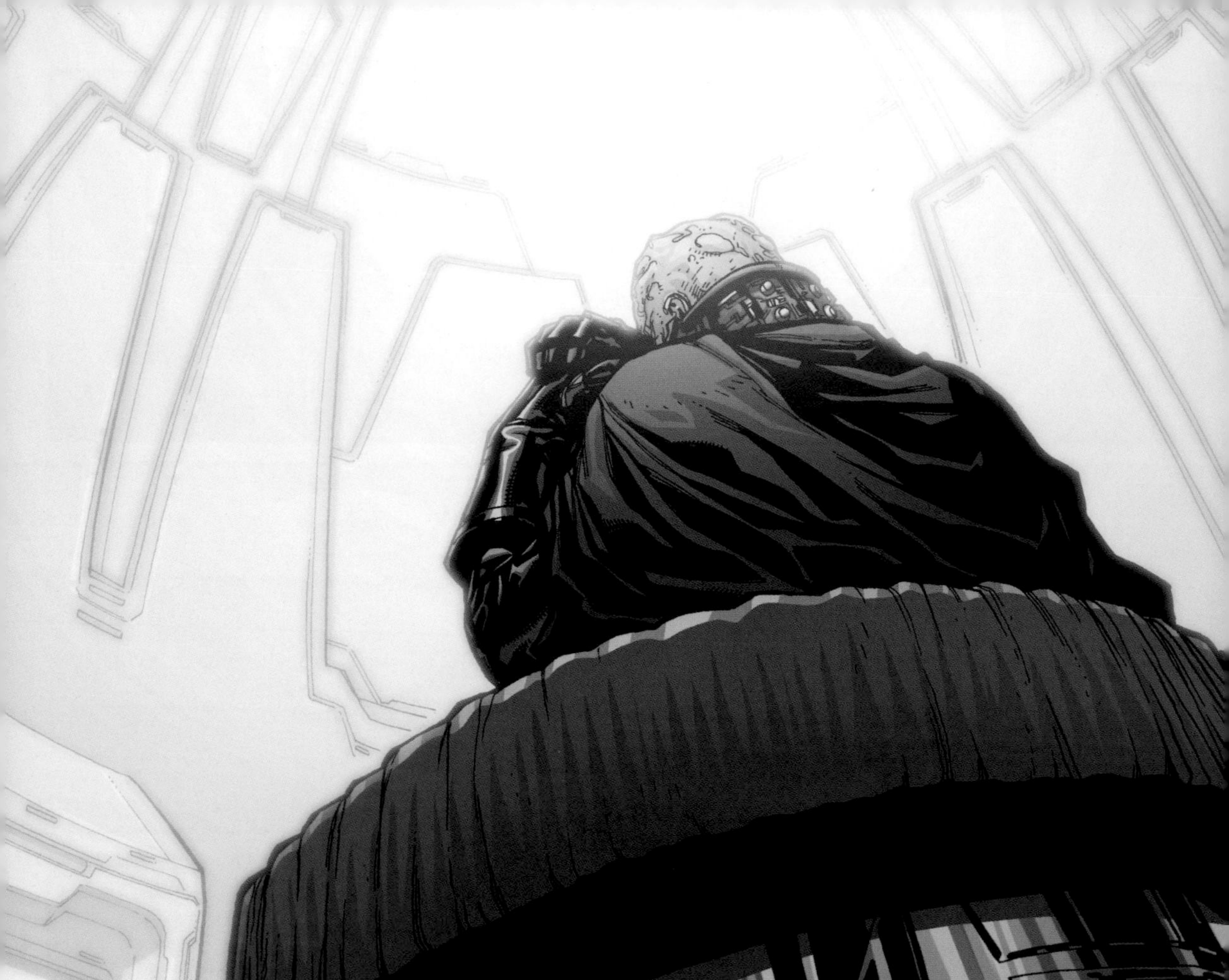
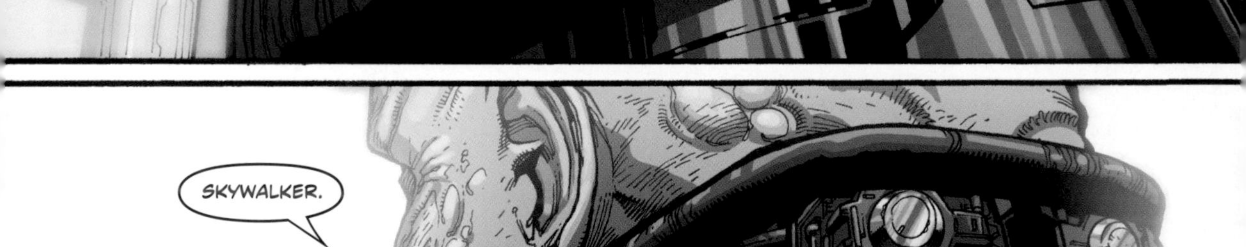
SKYWALKER.
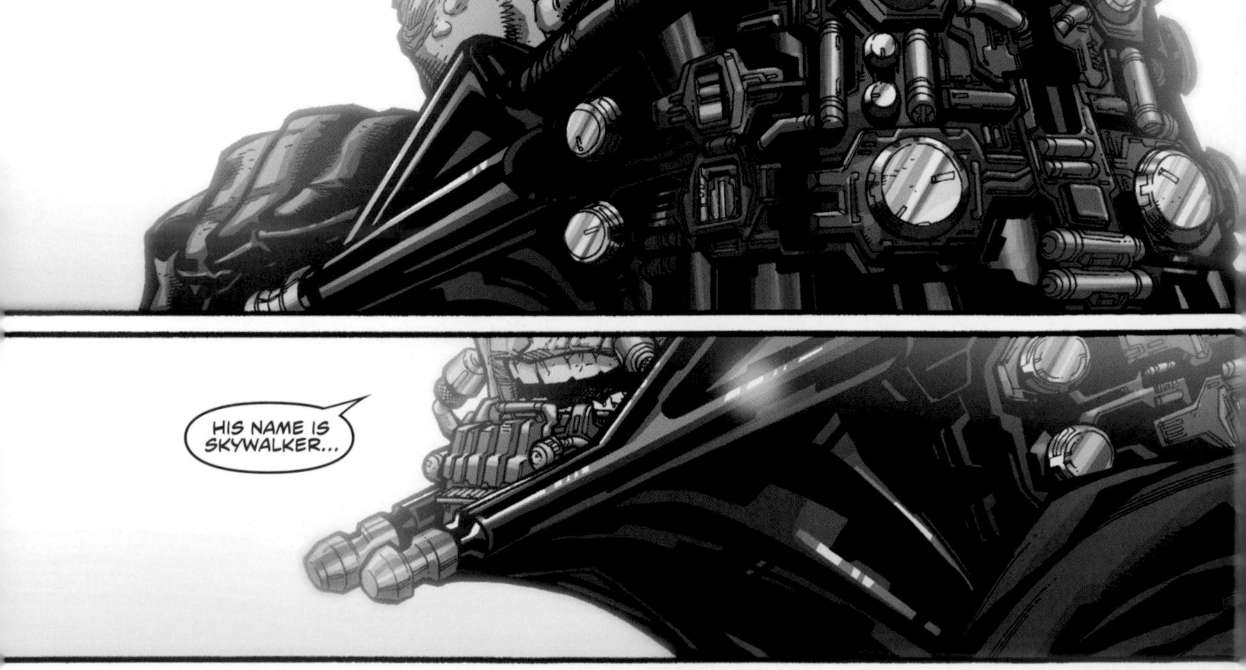
HIS NAME IS SKYWALKER...

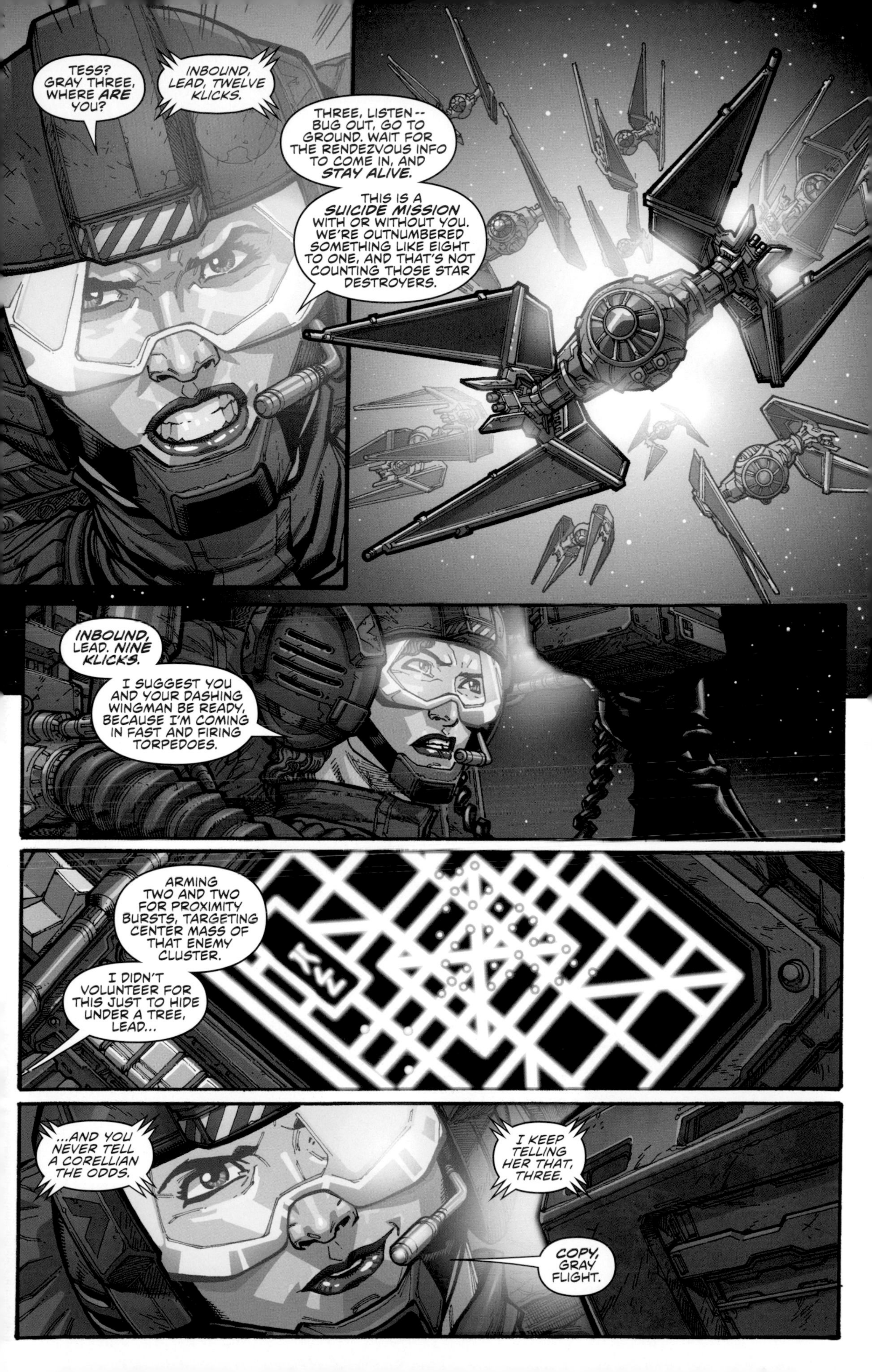
TESS? GRAY THREE, WHERE ARE YOU?
INBOUND, LEAD, TWELVE KLICKS.
THREE, LISTEN-- BUG OUT, GO TO GROUND. WAIT FOR THE RENDEZVOUS INFO TO COME IN, AND STAY ALIVE.
THIS IS A SUICIDE MISSION WITH OR WITHOUT YOU. WE'RE OUTNUMBERED SOMETHING LIKE EIGHT TO ONE, AND THAT'S NOT COUNTING THOSE STAR DESTROYERS.
INBOUND, LEAD. NINE KLICKS.
I SUGGEST YOU AND YOUR DASHING WINGMAN BE READY, BECAUSE I'M COMING IN FAST AND FIRING TORPEDOES.
ARMING TWO AND TWO FOR PROXIMITY BURSTS, TARGETING CENTER MASS OF THAT ENEMY CLUSTER.
I DIDN'T VOLUNTEER FOR THIS JUST TO HIDE UNDER A TREE, LEAD...
...AND YOU NEVER TELL A CORELLIAN THE ODDS.
I KEEP TELLING HER THAT, THREE.
COPY, GRAY FLIGHT.

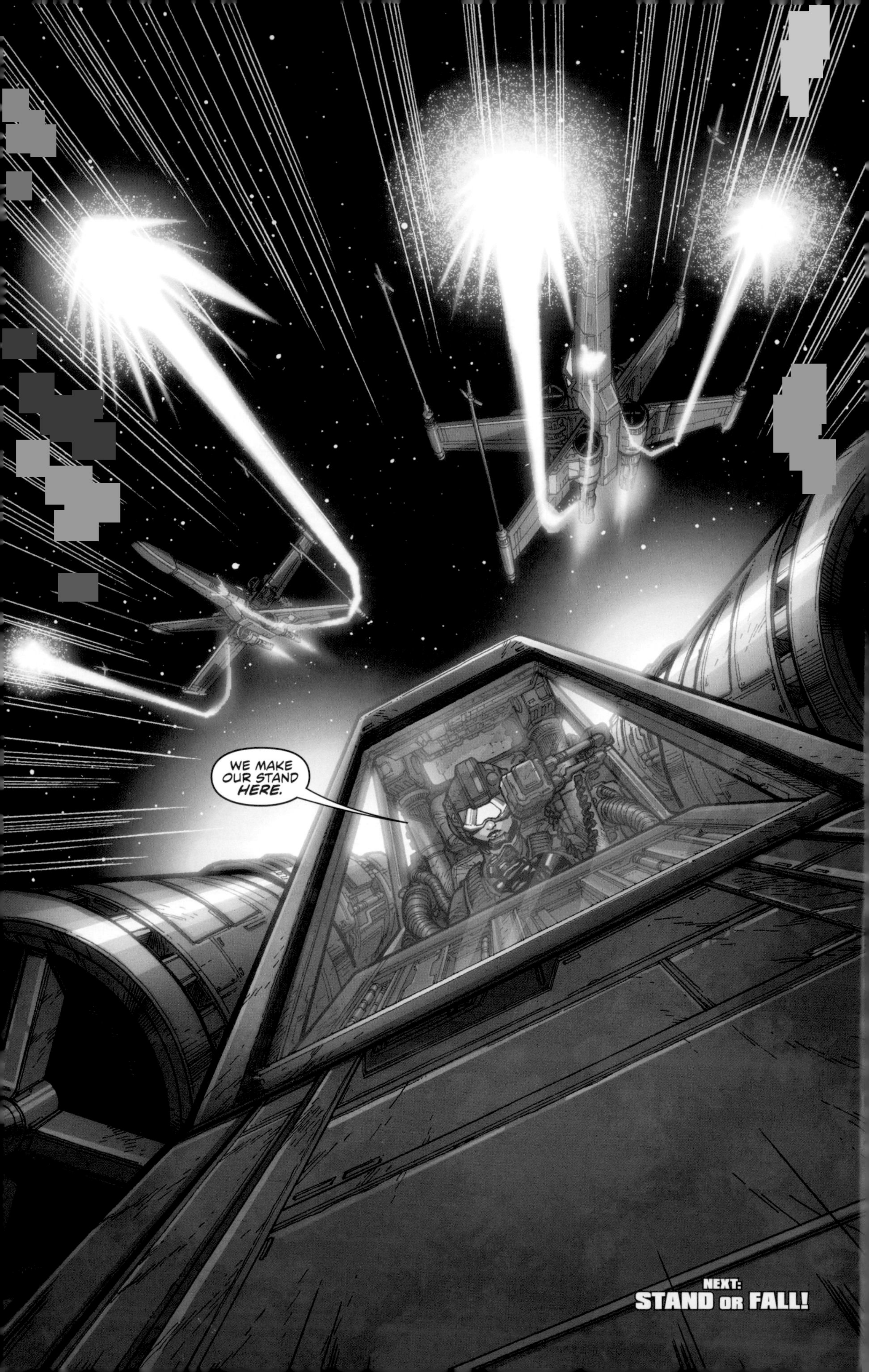
WE MAKE OUR STAND HERE.
NEXT:
STAND OR FALL!